Christmas Coloring

This book belongs to:

_____

MERRY CHRISTMAS

To:

From:

We create our books with great love and care yet mistakes beyond our control can happen in printing, binding and shipping. If you have any questions, comments, concerns, or problems with this book please contact us at: bluejewelbooks@gmail.com.

Published by Blue Jewel Books
Copyright © 2023

Merry Christmas

Merry Christmas

CHRISTMAS COUNTDOWN CALENDAR

Color and cut out your own gift tags.

To: _____
From: _____

To: _____
From: _____

Jingle Bells

To: _____
From: _____

To: _____
From: _____

Happy Holidays!

To: _____
From: _____

Peace & Joy

To: _____
From: _____

To: _____
From: _____

To: _____
From: _____

JOY

To: _____
From: _____

To: _____
From: _____

Merry Christmas!

To: _____
From: _____

Ho Ho Ho

To: _____
From: _____

Made in the USA
Monee, IL
04 November 2024

69286746R00063